LEVEL **2** READER

Shopkins™

Once you shop...You can't stop!

A VERY SHOPKINS VACATION

By Jenne Simon

SCHOLASTIC INC.

ISBN 978-1-338-10883-5

10 9 8 7 6 5 4 3 2 1   17 18 19 20 21

Printed in the U.S.A.   132

First printing 2017

Book design by Erin McMahon

"I am bored today," Cheeky Chocolate says to
ilk Bud.

Shopville is a great place to live. But Cheeky
ants to do something new.

"Time to plan my vacation!" she says.

All the Shopkins want to help.
Where should Cheeky go?

"I want an adventure," says Cheeky. "Where n I go to have lots of fun?"

"I have a cool idea," says Strawberry Kiss.
"How about a visit to the mountains?"

"Slick Breadstick went skiing last year," says
trawberry. "But you must be careful. He said
he ice can be very . . . well . . . slick!"

"Mountain climbing is a blast," Strawberry tells Cheeky. "But you need to be chill and have a fresh attitude to make it to the top!"

"A cozy log cabin in the mountains is the erfect place to get away," she adds.

"Br-r-r-rilliant!" says Cheeky, imagining herself in the snowy scene.

But then Cheeky's mind starts to run wild.

Strawberry has not mentioned any of the things that could go wrong.

Cheeky would have to watch out for snow-storms and freezer burn.

What if she gets a visit from a scary snow monster?

Cheeky freezes.

"I don't think this is the vacation for me after ll," she says.

"I have an idea," says Lippy Lips. She thinks Cheeky should visit the style capital of the world . . . Paris!

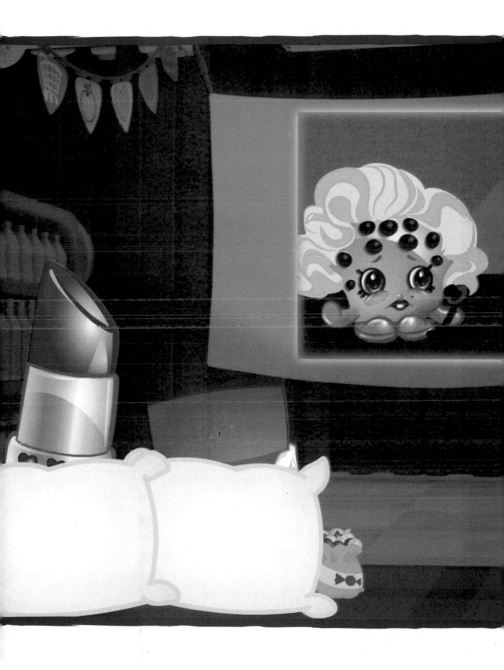

"You could go see a French film," Lippy tells heeky.

"Milk Bud could go with you! Paris is the perfect place to pamper your pet in style!" Lippy adds.

"But most importantly, you can shop till you
rop!" Lippy says. "You'll see all the hottest
shion shows!"

But Cheeky is not convinced.
Shopping for silly hats is not her idea of the perfect vacation.

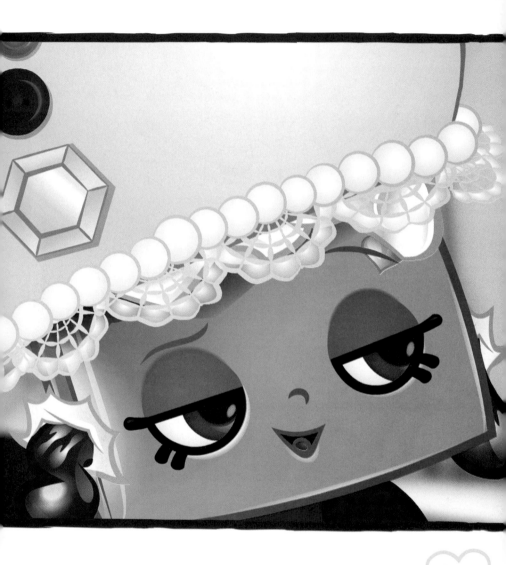

"I don't think that is the trip for me, either,"
ys Cheeky.

"Like, I've got the brightest idea," says Suzie Sundae. "A beach vay-kay is totally what you need."

"Imagine lying on a comfy chair with the
arm sun on your face," says Suzie.

"I don't know," Apple Blossom says. "The bea
is not all fun in the sun."

"It can get very hot," Apple warns Suzie.
What if you . . . melt?"

"Don't worry about that!" says Suzie. "At the beach you can, like, play in the sand and dig for buried treasure!"

"That *does* sound sweet," says Cheeky.

She could already feel the island breeze on her face!

But Apple Blossom is not finished trying to change Cheeky's mind.

"The sand may be safe, but do you know what lives in the sea?" asks Apple.

Cheeky shakes her head. "No, what?"

"Sea monsters!" Apple cries.

"Sea monsters aren't real, Apple," says Cheeky.

"It seems pretty risky," says Apple. "Are you sure that is the kind of vacation you want?"

"I'm not worried," says Cheeky. She is ready to go!

Cheeky does not believe in sea monsters, but she *does* believe she found the perfect vacation adventure.

As Cheeky starts to leave, two long, purple tentacles splash out of the fountain.

"What is that?" Cheeky cries, running to hide behind Strawberry Kiss.

Maybe sea monsters *do* exist!

Or maybe Kooky Cookie is trying to give heeky a little adventure right here at home in hopville!

With friends like the Shopkins, every day is an adventure!